Andy's Wild Animal Adventure

Andy's Wild Animal Adventure

By Gerda Marie Scheidl
Illustrated by Gisela Dürr

Translated by J. Alison James

North-South Books

NEW YORK / LONDON

First published in the United States, Great Britain, Canada,
Australia, and New Zealand in 1997 by North-South Books,
an imprint of Nord-Süd Verlag AG, Gossau Zürich, Switzerland.

Distributed in the United States by North-South Books Inc., New York.

Library of Congress Cataloging-in-Publication Data is available.
A CIP catalogue record for this book is available from The British Library.
ISBN 1-55858-797-7 (TRADE BINDING)
1 3 5 7 9 TB 10 8 6 4 2
ISBN 1-55858-798-5 (LIBRARY BINDING)
1 3 5 7 9 LB 10 8 6 4 2

Printed in Belgium

For more information about our books, and the authors and artists
who create them, visit our web site: http://www.northsouth.com

Last Saturday, Andy visited his aunt
Charlotte. He liked spending the day with
her. She had a wonderful garden to play
in. She made delicious food. But last
Saturday something special happened.

Tea Rice Suga

Everything started
in the usual way.
When he got there,
Aunt Charlotte was
busy cooking noodle
soup with meatballs.

She gave Andy a
sketch pad and a
handful of crayons.

"Will you draw me
a picture?" she said.
"I'd love a picture
with bright flowers
and maybe some
butterflies."

Flowers! Andy thought as he went out
into the garden. What a stupid thing to
draw! And butterflies, they were boring
too. He could think of something much
more exciting.

He didn't have to think long.

"I'll draw some wild animals," he said. Andy drew a lion. Lions are especially wild. At least the lion that Andy drew looked especially wild.

Andy glanced up from his drawing. He rubbed his eyes. What on earth was that?

Andy squeezed his eyes shut. He opened them again. The lion from the picture was right in front of Andy, sitting on the grass. A real, live lion.

"Are you a real lion?" asked Andy to
make sure.

"GRRROWWL . . ." snarled the lion,
and she swished her tail. Andy anxiously
pulled his legs in under him. That's a
real lion all right, he thought, and he
smiled at the lion carefully.

The lion stood up . . . and came closer.

And she rubbed her back against
Andy's legs.

Andy carefully stuck out his hand and
stroked the lion. He wasn't a bit afraid
now, so he gave the lion a big hug.

All of a sudden she jumped up next to
Andy on the bench, nestled tightly against
him, and started to purr.

"What are you up to, Andy?" called
Aunt Charlotte from the window.
"I'm playing with this lion," called
Andy.
"A lion?" asked Aunt Charlotte.

"First I drew a picture
of a lion. And now here
she is, sitting next to me."

"I see," said Aunt Charlotte.

"It's a real, live lion,"
said Andy.

Aunt Charlotte said,
"Real lions are dangerous.
Won't it bite?"

"No," said Andy.
"She is quite tame."

"Good enough, then,"
said Aunt Charlotte.
"Lunch isn't ready yet,
so you have time to
make one or two more
pictures. But please,
no more lions."

"What do you think I should draw now?" he asked the lion.

The lion yawned loudly and stepped down from the bench. She lay on the grass and fell asleep.

"You're no fun," Andy said. "I think I'll make an elephant to play with. Elephants aren't lazy."

Elephants are big and round and wrinkled. So Andy drew a big, round, wrinkled elephant.

Andy heard a snort from the garden path. He looked up from his picture and . . .

there stood a big, round, wrinkled elephant with giant floppy ears.

The elephant trotted over to the apple tree and picked an apple with his trunk. Smack, chomp, he ate the apple up. Then he ate another and another.

"Hey, stop that!" cried Andy. "What are you doing? Those are Aunt Charlotte's apples."

The elephant nudged Andy with his trunk.

"Okay," laughed Andy. "I guess you can have a few."

So the elephant helped himself to another apple.

"What are you up to, Andy?" called Aunt Charlotte.

"I'm playing with this elephant," answered Andy.

"An elephant?" asked Aunt Charlotte.

"Yes. I drew a picture of an elephant. And now here he is, picking your apples."

18

"My apples?" asked Aunt Charlotte.

"It's a real, live elephant," said Andy.

"Won't those apples make him sick?" Aunt Charlotte asked.

"No," said Andy. "Apples are good for elephants."

"Well, all right then."

Aunt Charlotte slipped the noodles into the soup. "You can draw one more picture, then it's time to eat," she called to Andy. "But please, no more elephants. I don't have enough apples."

One elephant is enough, thought Andy.
Besides, Andy wanted someone to play
with. The lion was lying in the grass,
sleeping. The elephant was picking apples
one by one and eating them, seeds and all.

"PIE-RAAT! PA-RAAT!" said the parrot.

Finally Andy understood. "Pirate! You're saying you're a pirate's parrot!" he cried.

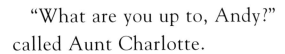

"What are you up to, Andy?" called Aunt Charlotte.

"I'm playing with this parrot."

"With what?" asked Aunt Charlotte.

"I drew a parrot, and now here he is, sitting on my shoulder," called Andy.

"I see," said his aunt.

"It's a real, live parrot. And he can even talk. He's a pirate's parrot!"

"Are you a hungry pirate?" asked Aunt Charlotte.

"Aye-aye, Captain!" called Andy.

"Then come on in. Lunch is ready."

"Can the parrot come?" asked Andy.

"Of course."

"And the lion, too?"

"If he doesn't make a mess."

"The lion is very polite. She will eat the soup with a spoon."

The parrot didn't like meatballs, but he enjoyed the noodles. He sat on the edge of the bowl and picked the noodles from the soup.

The lion liked the meatballs, so she ate the parrot's, too.

Then the elephant looked in through the window to see if they were finished. Andy jumped right up to go and play. The lion turned to go as well.

"Wait just one minute!" called Aunt Charlotte. "First finish eating. And then what about washing the dishes?"

"Yuck," said Andy. "I hate washing dishes." He sat down again.

"Washing dishes can be fun," said Aunt Charlotte.

Next to the window there was a big rain barrel. The elephant dipped his trunk deep into the water; then he stuck his trunk in through the window and sprayed the kitchen.

"What was that? You made us all wet!" cried Aunt Charlotte.

"He only wanted to help," said Andy. "You were right. Washing dishes *can* be fun."

Everyone got soaked.
The lion sprang up on the
table. The parrot flapped back
and forth and screeched.

"Stop! Stop at once!" cried
Aunt Charlotte.

But the elephant thought it
was funny and kept on spraying.

"This is not a game anymore!"
scolded Aunt Charlotte. "It's time
for these animals to disappear.
All three."

Suddenly it was quiet. "Where
should they disappear to?" asked
Andy softly.

"Maybe the zoo?"

"No, please not the zoo. They'd
get scared in the zoo," said Andy.

"Then you'll have to draw a cage out in the garden," said Aunt Charlotte.

Good idea, thought Andy.

He drew a cage.

A great big cage, so all the animals would have enough room.

Aunt Charlotte pushed them inside and shut the door. Now there was some peace and quiet.

But something was not right. The parrot squatted sadly on the ground. The lion sat in the corner and cried. And the elephant hung his ears and sniffled.

Andy sniffled too. He couldn't hold
back the tears.

"I guess the cage wasn't such a good idea
after all," said Andy.

"What are we going to do with them?" asked Aunt Charlotte.

Andy thought for a moment. "We could send them home."

"How?" asked Aunt Charlotte.

Andy laughed. "I'll just draw a jungle. And then the animals will disappear into it."

"Do you think that will work?"

"Let's see." Andy quickly got his crayons and his sketch pad, and drew a jungle. He painted immense trees and wonderful flowers blossoming among the greenery. The ground was covered with tall grass.

Andy drew and drew.

Suddenly he thought he saw a flash of red feathers perched in a palm. Then he saw a piece of the lion's tail, and noticed the elephant's back. Andy drew a giant fern over the lion's tail until it was gone. Now he could see only the floppy ears of the elephant. Andy drew a thick bush with his dark-green crayon, and the elephant disappeared too.

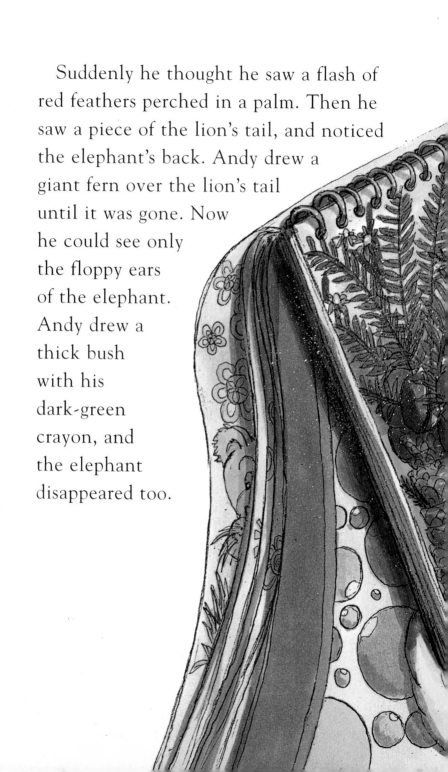

Andy ran to the cage. It was empty.
"It worked!" he cried.

But where had the parrot gone?

"Pirate parrot?" called Andy.

"PIE-RAAT!" came an answer from
far inside the jungle.

Then all was quiet. The cage, the jungle, the lion, the elephant, and the parrot had all disappeared.

"Good-bye, parrot," whispered Andy.

Andy was sad.

"It was only a game," comforted Aunt Charlotte.

"But the parrot . . ." said Andy.

His aunt laughed. "It was only a play parrot."

"And the lion? Only a play lion?"

"Yes, my sweet," said Aunt Charlotte, and took him in her arms. Then she saw the fire-red parrot feather in Andy's hand.

"Shall I draw new animals?"

"You'd better not," said Aunt Charlotte.

"How about if I draw you a picture with flowers and butterflies, like you asked?" said Andy.

"That sounds like a very good idea," Aunt Charlotte replied.

And that's just what Andy drew.

ABOUT THE AUTHOR

Gerda Marie Scheidl was born in a small town in Germany. She studied dance and acting in Vienna. She worked for many years as a dancer, and then became the manager of a children's theater. She was the stage director, designed the costumes and sets, and wrote the plays. Later she began writing fairy tales and children's books, including *Loretta and the Little Fairy* and *The Moon Man*, both published by North-South. She now lives near Hannover, Germany.

About the Illustrator

Gisela Dürr studied art at the University
of Applied Science in Mainz, Germany,
and did an academic exchange with an art
school in Zurich, Switzerland. Since then
she has illustrated numerous picture
books, including two North-South Books,
The Secret of Trembleton Hall and *Henry
and Horace Clean Up*. She lives in
Munich, Germany.